God's Easter Gifts

Written by
Brenda Castro

Designed by
Sherry Boas

Using illustrations from
various artists* including

...ria Boas

Caritas Press

*See back page

Early morning on Easter Sunday, Mrs. Diaz arranged white flowers in Bella's hair and helped Pablo put on his bow tie and shine his shoes. The children wanted to look their best on Easter Sunday to celebrate the life of Jesus. They were going to Holy Mass and then to an Easter egg hunt in the park.

The Church looked radiant with the light of Jesus, and the children knew God had prepared many gifts for them.

When Mass was over, Bella and Pablo shook hands with Father, gave him the Easter card they had colored for him and ran for the park.

The warm breeze brushed softly across the spring flowers, which were in full bloom, making the butterflies dance and the birds sing.

The children couldn't wait to begin. The Easter egg hunt was their favorite part of Easter.

The eggs were always filled with candy, toys, and goodies.

But Mr. Diaz explained to Bella and Pablo that there is more to Easter than candy. The children were about to go on a very special Easter egg hunt. Soon they would understand God's love for them and all the great gifts He has given the world.

Bella was the first to find an egg. Nestled in the grass near an arbor, it was the most beautiful egg she and Pablo had ever seen. It was decorated with bright pink roses.

When Bella opened it, the children discovered one of God's greatest gifts.

THE GIFT OF STRENGTH

Jesus had the strength to fast for forty days and forty nights in the desert. Ash Wednesday is the beginning of our forty days of Lent, a time that we do hard things so we can become stronger in our love for God. Angels came to comfort Jesus during his time in the desert, just as our guardian angels comfort and strengthen us during times of trouble. We are grateful for the strength God gives us to endure day-to- day problems and the difficult things we must face in life.

When have you had to be strong?

Bella and Pablo ran on to find more eggs. The girl noticed something turquoise and coral hidden in a tuft of grass under a park bench. It was another egg!

Bella handed it to her brother. When Pablo opened it, the children were amazed to learn of another great gift from God.

THE GIFT OF NATURE

Jesus was honored with palm branches when he rode a donkey into Jerusalem to begin his suffering and die for us.

We all enjoy God's creation — the very beautiful gifts of nature God has given us. He has blessed us with trees, flowers, oceans and mountains. He has given us wild animals to amaze us and pets to keep us company.

What is your favorite part of nature?

As they continued their Easter egg hunt, Bella spotted an egg that looked like one of grandma's quilts. It was hiding in the grass under a swing. She opened it immediately and was delighted to see what was inside.

THE GIFT OF FRIENDSHIP

Jesus had many friends and followers. His closest friends were his apostles. They went everywhere with him. Jesus showed them how to be a true friend when he washed Peter's feet at the Last Supper. He showed his friends we should serve one another.

How do you serve your friends?

Bella and Pablo had a feeling there would be an egg hiding somewhere in the tall grass that fringed the sparkling pond. Bella searched on the north side and Pablo took the south. It wasn't long before Bella heard her brother call out. He had found another one of God's gifts.

THE GIFT OF FOOD

Before Jesus died for our sins, he had his last meal with the twelve apostles. This is known as The Last Supper, and it is celebrated on Holy Thursday, on the week before Easter. During the meal, Jesus told His disciples that he would give his body and blood to help us live a holy life and get to heaven.

One time, Jesus taught His friends to pray "give us this day our daily bread." This prayer reminds us that Jesus not only gives us His body and blood to nourish our souls, but God also provides all the food that we enjoy every day. Because He has blessed us with this gift, we are happy to give thanks to the Lord at mealtimes.

What is your favorite food?

The children continued their search. It wasn't long before they found another egg, nestled in a flower box on the bridge. When they opened the egg, they found an amazing gift.

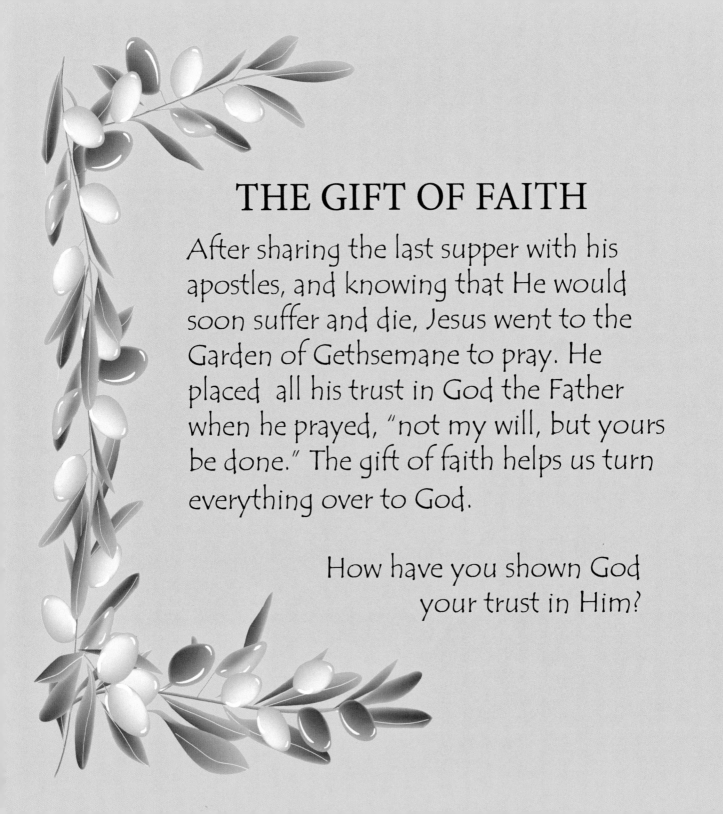

THE GIFT OF FAITH

After sharing the last supper with his apostles, and knowing that He would soon suffer and die, Jesus went to the Garden of Gethsemane to pray. He placed all his trust in God the Father when he prayed, "not my will, but yours be done." The gift of faith helps us turn everything over to God.

How have you shown God your trust in Him?

Just over the bridge, the children came to a meadow. Hiding behind a tree, was a light green egg with gold trim.

When Bella opened it, the children found a wonderful surprise.

THE GIFT OF FAMILY

When Jesus was arrested and sentenced to death on Good Friday, His mother Mary was right by His side the whole time. God has blessed us with family to love us, play with us and take care of us.

What are some of the ways your family shows love for one another?

The children were happy that their basket was full, and their tummies were rumbling with the thought of the great Easter feast their family had planned after the Easter egg hunt. But Mrs. Diaz told them there was one more egg yet to be found.

This one is the
greatest gift
of all, and the
children found it
nestled in some
tall grass.

THE GIFT OF LIFE

After Jesus died on the cross, he was buried in a tomb and came back to life in three days. This is why we celebrate Easter! By His death and resurrection, Jesus opened Heaven for us, so we can all live forever with God, in complete happiness.

We are grateful that God loved us so much that He gave us life and sent His Son to save us and lead us to Heaven.

What are all the things you are thankful for in your life?

That Easter, Bella and Pablo discovered that the most important part of Easter is not the candy or the toys. They learned that Easter is about celebrating all the many gifts God gave us, especially the gift of His Son, Jesus.

For my husband, Leo. Thank you for always believing in me.
For the three greatest gifts God has given me: David, Valeria, and Pablo.
You are my life!
—Brenda Castro

GOD'S EASTER GIFTS
Copyright © 2014 Brenda Castro
Printed in the USA

First Edition
10 9 8 7 6 5 4 3 2 1
ISBN: 978-1-940209-13-5

Contact Sherry@LilyTrilogy.com

Artwork

Bella and Pablo, Madonna and Child in church: Maria Boas

Remaining Illustrations purchased from Fotolia.com:
© Sweet Angel © Anatolii © ilolab © alenalihacheva © annamei © Andreev-studio © svetavo © 8meg © Carlos Santa Maria © Matthew Cole © karandaev © michael715 © Alexander Potapov © minimus © agawa288 © jimlarkin © Africa Studio © Renáta Sedmáková © kubais © milovelen © justdd © skywing © annamei © 31moonlight31 © baoyan © susanafh © mythja © pr2is © Mariia Pazhyna

Classic Artwork in the Public Domain: Angels ministering to Christ in the Wilderness by Thomas Cole, Entry into Jerusalem by Anonymous (Gdansk), Christ washing Peter's feet by Giovanni Antonio Sogliani, Christ in Gethsemane by Heinrich Hofmann, Last Supper by Juan de Juanes

ABOUT CARITAS PRESS

Caritas Press was founded in 2011 with the mission of shedding light on things eternal in a culture that is becoming increasingly blind to the wonders of God's works and numb to His boundless love. Making use of the subtle and the beautiful, Caritas Press hopes to play a part in igniting in children and adults a desire to know God more fully. Other children's books available from Caritas Press include *Victoria's Sparrows, Miraculous Me, Barnyard Bliss* and *Billowtail*. For a full listing of all Caritas titles for children, youths and adults, visit CaritasPress.org.

ARCHANGELA'S HORSE

Archangela comes to understand God's will when her beloved and loyal horse refuses to take her where she wants to go.
By Sherry Boas

SAINT JOHN BOSCO AND HIS BIG GRAY DOG

Colorfully-illustrated story of a special canine guardian who came to St. John Bosco's aid whenever he was in danger. By Hayley Madieros

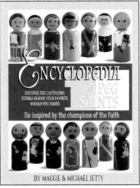

ENCYCLOPEDIA OF PEG SAINTS

Get to know 36 saints in an engaging and easy to "absorb" format, centered around colorful hand-painted peg dolls collected and cherished by Catholic kids everywhere. By Maggie & Michael Jetty

ARABEL'S LAMB

A young girl's compassion is tested to the limits in this gripping tale about love and sacrifice. Children will cheer as George defeats the dragon. By Sherry Boas

JACKIE'S SPECIAL HALLOWEEN

Sister and brother duo Bella and Pablo return in another delightful story by Brenda Castro.

MIRACULOUS ME

A mother and father dream of the future as they celebrate the precious gift of life, the baby who is about to arrive. What will the days of her life hold? By Ruth Pendergast Sissel & Tina Tolliver Matney

BARNYARD BLISS

All of creation rejoices as word of the baby owlet spreads throughout the farm from one animal to the next. By Ruth Pendergast Sissel & Tina Tolliver Matney

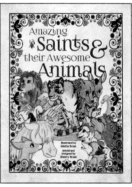

AMAZING SAINTS & THEIR AWESOME ANIMALS

Every animal is sure to love this collection of saint stories . By Sherry Boas

BILLOWTAIL

Little creatures on a big adventure in medieval Spain! 220-page Novel.
By Sherry Boas

VICTORIA'S SPARROWS

A sweet story that shows the beauty of God's providence and how much He cares for us.
By Sherry Boas

THE GIFT IN THE MANGER

When their feeding trough ends up serving as a bed for a tiny baby, the animals get a glimpse into God's loving plan to save the world. Like every one of us, each of the animals gathered around the manger has a struggle to overcome. They, like us, find the answer in Jesus, the only one who can fix our brokenness, heal our imperfections and give us the gift that makes us whole – the gift of Himself.
By Sherry Boas

CaritasPress.org

Made in the USA
Monee, IL
07 April 2022

94275218R00029